for Stan
V. F.
for Amelia Edwards
with love and gratitude
D. K.

First published 2002 by Walker Books Ltd
87 Vauxhall Walk, London SE11 5HJ

This edition published 2006

10 9 8 7 6 5 4 3 2 1

Text © 2002 Vivian French
Illustrations © 2002 Dana Kubick

The right of Vivian French and Dana Kubick to be
identified as author and illustrator respectively of
this work has been asserted by them in accordance
with the Copyright, Designs and Patents Act 1988

This book has been typeset in Minion Condensed

Printed in China

British Library Cataloguing in Publication Data:
a catalogue record for this book is available
from the British Library

ISBN-13: 978-1-4063-0152-6
ISBN-10: 1-4063-0152-3

To Mum With Love

Written by
Vivian French

Illustrated by
Dana Kubick

WALKER BOOKS
AND SUBSIDIARIES
LONDON · BOSTON · SYDNEY · AUCKLAND

It was the day before
Mum's birthday.
Stanley went to see
his big brother, Rex.

"What are you giving
Mum?" he asked.
"Flowers," said Rex.
"She likes flowers."

"Good idea,"
said Stanley,
and he hurried
off to the
garden.

Good idea

Stanley picked ... five of the biggest ...

...lowers ...   that he could see ...

but by the time
he got back inside,
all the petals
had fallen off.
"Bother," said
Stanley, and his
ears drooped.

– Bother

Stanley went to find
his big sister, Queenie.
She was counting the
money in her money-box.
"Is that for Mum's
present?" Stanley asked.
"Yes," said Queenie.
"I'm giving her
a tin of toffees."

"Oh," said Stanley,
and he rushed
off to find his
own money-box.

-Oh!

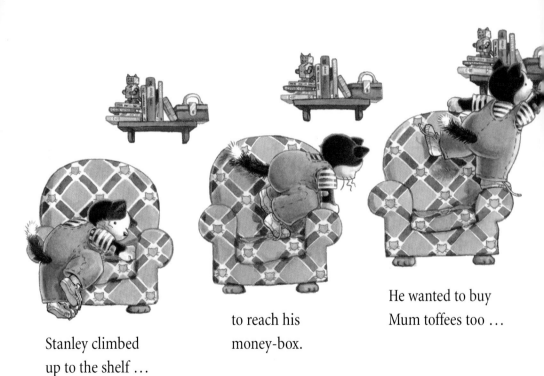

Stanley climbed
up to the shelf …

to reach his
money-box.

He wanted to buy
Mum toffees too …

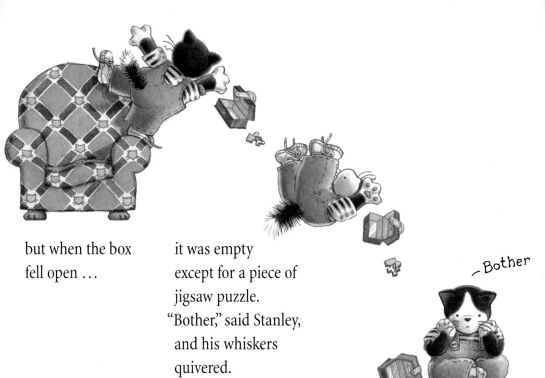

but when the box fell open …

it was empty except for a piece of jigsaw puzzle. "Bother," said Stanley, and his whiskers quivered.

– Bother

Stanley went to look for
his biggest sister, Flora.
"What are you doing?"
he asked.
"Making Mum a birthday
cake," Flora said.

"Hurrah!" said Stanley, and he dashed out of the kitchen.

–Hurrah!

 Stanley's mud cake …  looked …

lovely ...

Bother

but not for long.
"Bother," said
Stanley, and
his tail dragged
behind him.

Stanley went slowly
upstairs to look for
a present for Mum.
He tipped out his
cardboard box of cars,
but there was nothing
that wasn't chipped
or dented.
Flora appeared in the
doorway. "Mum says
it's bedtime," she said.

That night, Stanley
didn't sleep very well.

Early next morning, Flora,
Queenie and Rex came into
Stanley's room.
"What's the matter?" Rex asked.
"I haven't got anything for
Mum," said Stanley.
"Just give her a kiss,"
said Flora. "That's
what she'd
like best."

Stanley sat bolt upright.
"I know!" he said.
"I know what to do."
"Are you coming?" said Queenie.
"In a minute," Stanley said.

Flora, Queenie and Rex
went downstairs to give
Mum their presents.

"Flowers!" said Mum. "They're lovely! And my favourite toffees! And WHAT a beautiful cake – but where's Stanley?"

Suddenly …

Stanley was standing
in the doorway,
carrying his big
cardboard box.
"HAPPY BIRTHDAY!"
he said.

Mum began to open the box. "Stanley!" said Rex and Flora and Queenie. "There's nothing inside!"

To Mum

"Yes there is!" said Stanley.
"It's a box of kisses!
  And I filled it right up
  to the top!"
"Oh Stanley," said Mum, "it's
  a wonderful present," and
  she kissed Stanley's nose.
"Don't use them up all at
  once," said Rex.
  Mum smiled. "I think boxes
  of kisses last for ever
  and ever," she said.

"Yes," said
Stanley.
"For ever
and ever
and EVER."
But he
gave Mum
another kiss –
just in case.